AN UNOFFICIAL **MINECRAFT** BOOK

DIARY OF A
MINECRAFT
WOLF

© 2023 Scholastic Australia

First published by Scholastic Australia Pty Limited in 2023.

All rights reserved. Published by Scholastic Inc., *Publishers since 1920*. SCHOLASTIC and associated logos are trademarks and/or registered trademarks of Scholastic Inc.

The publisher does not have any control over and does not assume any responsibility for author or third-party websites or their content.

This book is a work of fiction. Names, characters, places, and incidents are either the product of the author's imagination or are used fictitiously, and any resemblance to actual persons, living or dead, business establishments, events, or locales is entirely coincidental.

ISBN 978-1-339-04123-0

10 9 8 7 6 5 4 3 2 1   24 25 26 27 28

Printed in the U.S.A.   132

This edition first printing, April 2024

Cover design by Hannah Janzen and Ashley Vargas

Internal design by Hannah Janzen

Typeset in KG First Time in Forever, More Sugar, and White NT

DIARY *OF A* MINECRAFT

WOLF

UNDERWATER HEIST

SCHOLASTIC INC.

MONDAY

Bored, bored, BORED! **A THOUSAND TIMES BORED!** Ever since I completed my first secret agent mission, life as a regular Minecraft wolf has seemed so dull.

Patrolling the Den where my pack lives—**boring.** Chasing my tail—**boring.** Even hanging out with the other wolf recruits isn't as fun since I've become a **secret agent.**

On my last mission, I'd rescued my friends from a trap set by some **VILLAINOUS BABY TURTLES**—you know, the most evil things in all the Overworld—but because the baby turtles had hypnotized them with their cuteness, none of the recruits remembered how **heroic** I'd been! They don't remember the turtles at all, and whenever I try to remind them, they think that I'm imagining things.

Besides, we are on different **career paths** now. Most wolves my age are training to become GUARDs, the most elite group of wolves in Minecraft. But I am the **VERY FIRST** wolf to become a secret agent. And pretty soon I will have loads of missions under my collar.

"Any new missions yet, Winston?" Lobo laughed. "Or are you too busy daydreaming about baby turtles?"

I just stuck my nose in the air and trotted off. Those turtles would have done terrible things to him and the other recruits if I hadn't shown up! One day I'll have my proof. All I needed was another **mission** . . .

But the other wolves were far from supportive. I tried looking for new missions in creative places, but they all kept saying stuff like, "Hey! What are you doing **digging up** my garden?!" and

"AAGH! THERE'S A WET WOLF IN MY BATHTUB!"

They clearly didn't **understand.**
A secret agent's work can come
at **unexpected times** and in
unexpected places. Kind of like
GUARD duties.

GUARD stands for Guardians United
Against Real Dangers, and wolves
who join this force travel all over
Minecraft to **PATROL** biomes
for trouble, **PROTECT** villagers
and other mobs from players, and
GATHER INTEL on player activity.

What they don't do is **investigate,**
which is exactly why I became
a secret agent. My mission is to

uncover the **terrible truth** and expose Minecraft's most evil villains— **THE BABY TURTLES.**

And let's be real here—being a secret agent is the **coolest job EVER.**

"Real estate agent, was it?" said old Mrs. Lonewolf when I stopped to chat with her outside her cave. She squinted at me through her glasses while she watered her wolfsbane flowers. "Your mom said you're working with baby turtles, or something?"

"I'm not working *with* baby turtles,"

I said crossly. "I'm working *against* them."

"Well, good for you," she said. "I was wondering how you were going to **sell houses to turtles** when they already carry their homes around on their backs!"

"What?" I asked, frowning.

"Isn't that what real estate agents do? Sell houses?"

I sighed and explained the difference between a real estate agent and a secret agent to her.

She just smiled and patted me on the head, so I gave up. But after I left her, I  found myself thinking about what she'd said. Turtles *do* carry their homes around on their backs. Which means they could camp out on missions a lot longer than other mobs, biding their time until they could **strike.** I was really going to have to keep my eye out for that **SNEAKY MOB!**

It would help if I weren't so **alone** in my objective. But there was only one other being who understood the danger.

On my first mission, I'd found and **tamed** a player I'd named **Brian**, and he helped me defeat the baby turtles in battle so I could free my fellow wolves. But he'd disappeared right after the fight and I hadn't seen him since. I'm not even sure what to call him. My **pet?** My **friend?** He was very good with his sword, and with a bit more training, he might make a great secret agent one day. For now, he could just be my **JUNIOR PARTNER.**

He was also a **SECRET.** The other
wolves are suspicious of players, so
I hadn't told anyone that I'd tamed
one. My mom and the other GUARDs
believe that players are **trouble,**
and they usually blame players for
all the problems they encounter
in the Overworld. If they wouldn't
believe me about the baby turtles
being criminal masterminds, they
sure wouldn't believe that players
could be the good guys. So Brian has
to stay a secret . . . for now.

"Winston, are you chewing the rug again?!"

"**Oops**—sorry, Mom! I'm just so BORED!"

I was in my mom's office at work, trying to keep myself from **going insane** with boredom. I *still* didn't have a new mission. And, well, I *am* a wolf—I see a shoe, a newspaper, or a rug and I can't help but chew on it. It's a **canine thing.**

"Well, don't take it out on my workspace," Mom said. She was busy reading reports from the GUARDs out on assignments all over Minecraft. Some, from the Strike Force, were involved in **battles,** usually against players. Others, from the Intelligence division, were **observing** different biomes and sending back their findings. Most of the reports, however, were from the Security Squad, who were **patrolling** different areas to watch out for any **signs of trouble.**

"What *else* can I do?"

"Why don't you make yourself useful and monitor the **BARK radar?**"

That's the **Big Audio Relay Kit radar.** Glad for something to do and always happy to help my mom, I sat down in front of the large machine that picked up ultrasonic signals from wolves patrolling all over. Mobs could also contact the GUARDs through the BARK radar, requesting wolf help to **protect** villages or other locations from danger. As a **VIC—VERY IMPORTANT CANINE**—my mom had her own radar, and right now it was getting a faint reading.

"There's a message!" I said excitedly. I turned one of the knobs to make the sound clearer. "It says . . . **bark bark . . . bark-bark-bark bark . . . bark bark-bark** . . . Oh wow, this message is from the Drowned! They're requesting **urgent** GUARD assistance!"

"That again," Mom sighed. "This is their third message today. I told them that GUARDs are **highly specialized** wolves who can help with three things: strike attacks, security and protection, and intelligence gathering. Instead, they want us to investigate a **crime,** but they won't even tell me what happened! It's **SENSITIVE INFORMATION,** apparently." She shook her head. "GUARDs are not undercover investigators. I offered to send a squad for protection, but they said it would be too obvious having law enforcement roaming around. I don't think we can help."

"Excuse me, High Commander Wolf?" said a GUARD, politely pawing at the door. "It's time for your meeting."

My mom, Wendy Wolf, is one of the three high commanders of the **HOWL—High Order of Wolf Leadership—Council.** They run things around here and keep the pack in line. Everyone listens to my mom and thinks she's a **VIC** because she's one of the best GUARDs the Den has ever seen. But I listen to her and think she's a VIC because she's **MY MOM.** She might not believe me about the baby turtles, but she **believes *in* me,** and that's even more important.

"I'll be back in a little while, Winston," she said as she left.

On her chest, her **BADGES OF HONOR** gleamed in the cave light. Then I was alone in her office, with the options of either continuing to chew the rug or monitoring the BARK radar.

I chose the BARK radar.

The messages from the Drowned city were still coming in. Whoever was requesting help was getting **really desperate.** They needed someone to **investigate** and didn't know whom else to turn to, but Mom had said the GUARDs weren't able to assist.

Wait a minute . . .

Guardians United Against Real
Dangers might not be investigators,
**BUT SECRET AGENTS
DEFINITELY ARE!**

I activated the BARK radar's
microphone.

"Bark-bark
bark!"
I said.
"Can you
please give
me more
information?"

For a moment, there was silence at the other end. Then I got my answer.

"Bark, there's been a **robbery,** bark," came the reply.

The Drowned at the other end wasn't actually speaking our wolf language, but the radar picked up all kinds of correspondence across Minecraft and **translated** it into wolfspeak. It's a sophisticated dialect.

"A very special bark-bark-item has been **stolen** and we need bark-help to find the robbers. We are also bark-worried the same thieves will come back for another bark-bark-**treasure** that is very important to us."

An unsolved mystery! AN ENDANGERED TREASURE!

This.

Was.

A.

MISSION!

"Bark-bark bark, we're sending our **top agent**," I said into the microphone. Then I did an excited paw pump. **YES!** Finally, I had a mission!

I asked the Drowned for details about where to go, then I printed out a map, ran out the door, and . . . almost **crashed** smack-bang into my mom.

"Winston! What are you—"

"Mom! I've got a **new case!**" I exclaimed. "I'm heading off on an important mission. **Byeeeeee!**"

I started to dash away, but Mom **caught me** by the scruff of my neck.

"That's great," she said. "You can leave first thing in the morning. *After* you tell me **where you're going.**"

I whistled as I strolled through the jungle biome. The morning sun was shining, the parrots were singing, and I had a **new mission!**

I was wearing my invisible high-tech suit. Most wolves don't bother with fancy technology, but lately I've become a bit more **modern.** Just before my last mission, I met Edwina—she's an invention engineer—

who gave me a bunch of neat tech that really saved my furry behind during my battle against the baby turtles. Since then, there is *no way* I would go anywhere without my camouflaged armor or my Anti-ADORBS collar to help repel **baby turtle hypnosis.**

BANG. BANG. BANG.

I was nearly at the ocean biome when I heard the unmistakable sound of someone **building.** Only players ever bothered to build things in Minecraft. I'm not sure why, but they always feel

the need to punch down trees
or dig up minerals to use in their
constructions. So annoying.

Following the sounds, I peeked
between some trees and guess
whom I saw?

"BRIAN!"

My tamed player looked up. He was
holding a door in his hands and was
just about to stick it onto a wall.

"Winston?"

"What are you doing here?" I asked

excitedly. "I wasn't sure I'd ever find you again. Did you get **lost** after our battle with the baby turtles?"

"Huh? Lost?" Brian frowned.

"Yeah. You **disappeared,** Brian. I know sometimes pets wander off . . ."

"Here we go with the 'tamed player' thing again," he muttered. "I'm *not* your **pet,** Winston. I disappeared because I **stopped playing.** And my name isn't 'Brian.' That's just what *you* decided to call me. It's actually—"

"Yes, yes, Brian!" I said loudly, because players clearly were not very good **LISTENERS!** I'd have to keep training him. "I'm on a new mission to help the Drowned with an investigation and I could really use my **junior partner** on this one."

I thought he was going to argue some more—players are also **very stubborn**—but he looked **curious.**

"The Drowned? I was just reading about them this morning."

"Really?" Who knew players could read? "What did it say?"

"That they're **hostile mobs** who spawn in water biomes, or when a zombie drowns," Brian said. "They can't go in the sun and they carry **TRIDENTS**."

"Hmm, tridents," I said. "Like the baby turtles had when we faced them."

"And normally *only* Drowned carry tridents, so it was **very strange** that the baby turtles had them," Brian said. He looked at his half-built house. "I guess I could come help you investigate."

"Great!" We started walking.

"Uh, Brian? Are you going to carry that door the whole way?"

He tried a couple of times to put down the door, but it **remained** under his arm.

"Must be **glitching**," he said. "I'm sure I'll work out how to get rid of it on the way."

He didn't. By the time we reached the water's edge, Brian was in a **cranky mood.**

"I must have clicked **TEN THOUSAND TIMES!**" he said crossly, still holding the door under his arm.

"I'm not sure how clicking is going to help you put the door down,"

I admitted, "but anyway, here we are! Now we just have to swim down to the **UNDERWATER RUINS**. That's where the message on the BARK radar said to go. **But how do we breathe?**"

While Brian wrestled with his door, I started pressing buttons on my tech suit for something that could help me breathe underwater. Teleportation—nope. Invisibility—nope. Oh, maybe this one here? An **air bubble** grew around my head like a **helmet.** I stuck my head in the water and took a deep breath. **PERFECT!**

"Hey, Brian, look at this!" I said, bounding over excitedly. He was still struggling with his door, so when I **leaped** onto his back, I guess he lost his balance. He **fell face-first** into the water, the door held out in front of him. It slipped below the surface and got stuck in the sand. In the strangest **twist of luck,** a column of air appeared behind the door. It was the perfect size for Brian to stand up in and **TAKE A FEW BREATHS UNDERWATER!**

"Huh, I guess the walk–through videos were right," he said, staring down at the door beneath the water. "I'll have to bring this door with me to keep playing."

"This isn't a *game*, Brian. This investigation is **serious.** But if that door helps you breathe underwater, then—hey, where did it go?"

Brian had picked it up, and **IT HAD DISAPPEARED!** My jaw hung open.

"It's just in my inventory," he explained, which I think means he's **a bit magical. WOW!** I really chose a great player to be **MY PET!**

We dove under the water and swam to the bottom. My tech suit and Brian's door trick both worked great! We stayed close to the seafloor so that Brian could keep **whipping out** his door to place it on the sand. That way, he could hop into the air bubble it created and take a few deep breaths before **magicking** the door away "into his inventory" again, whatever *that* meant, and continue to swim. It wasn't as elegant as my **bubble helmet** but was almost as effective.

Eventually, we approached a huge structure surrounded by a **moat**

of lava. The Underwater Ruins was an impressive place to turn into a city. As we got closer, we could see **TWO FIERCE-LOOKING DROWNED** armed with tridents guarding the front archway.

"The city's closed to outsiders," one of them said when we tried to pass.

They **barred our way** with their tridents.

I **GULPED.** These were scary dudes!

"I thought the Drowned called for assistance from a secret agent?" Brian challenged.

"**BRIAN!** That's supposed to be a *secret!*" I hissed, nudging him.

"Oh, *you're* the secret agents? Why didn't you say so?" And they let us in.

"Good work, Brian. I was just about to say that," I said.

The Underwater Ruins was like a huge **stone maze,** except filled with water and with Drowned wandering around on their daily business. Drowned shopping for groceries. Drowned carrying library book bags. Drowned taking their kids to the park. It was weird, but it **reminded me of the Den.**

A strangely friendly-looking Drowned wearing a security badge approached us.

"I'm **Donny,** head of security," he said. "I'm **confused.** I was not expecting the GUARDs to send a wolf cub and a player."

At first I felt annoyed, but then I reminded myself that it wasn't his fault. Nobody **knew** what a secret agent was supposed to look like—I was the **FIRST ONE** in Minecraft!

"We are, in fact, secret agents," I started, "and even though—"

"Oh! And you're only *disguised* as a cub and a player. Well, that's **very clever**—I never would have guessed. Okay, come with me for a tour of the city, and I'll explain what's going on."

We followed Donny through some tunnels. Brian had to stop and dump his door on the seafloor a couple of times for air as we wandered. **Not weird at all.**

"One of the Drowned's most important artifacts was **stolen** recently," Donny explained anxiously. "We haven't told the general public because we don't want them to panic, but it's also why we didn't want GUARDs patrolling the area—mobs would know something was wrong."

"What was stolen?" Brian asked.

"Yes, good work, Brian! I was just about to ask that!" I said, starting to get annoyed.

Donny lowered his voice to a whisper.

"It was our **ENCHANTED BOOK,**" he said. "We caught the player responsible, but she doesn't have the item, so now we are worried there are **more criminals** hidden somewhere in the city."

"You *already* caught someone?!" Oh no! This mystery was already halfway solved **WITHOUT ME.**

"If we don't figure out how she got the book and where her accomplices are, I'm afraid they might return for another **very precious secret item,**" Donny went on. We stopped in front of a huge, locked door that looked like a vault. "Some of my team think the player might be **innocent,** but until we know *this* item is safe, I'm not taking the risk and she is staying in **jail.** Also . . . are you going to do that all day?"

Brian had just taken out his door and stuck it into the sand to breathe in its air bubble again.

"That's the plan," he said. "I really like breathing."

"Why didn't you say so? Here." Donny held a little token out to Brian.

"Hey, thanks! It's the

SLEEPING WITH THE FISHES ACHIEVEMENT!

Now I'll be able to breathe underwater all day!"

"What's the other item, Donny?" I interrupted. "Is it inside this **vault?**"

"Yes," Donny said, "and it's **a secret,** so I'm afraid I can't tell you." He swam off to continue the tour, waving for us to follow.

I looked over at Brian. This was shaping up to be a **VERY FISHY MYSTERY** after all!

When our tour of the city ended, I asked Donny to show us the scene of the crime. The Drowned seemed to have **two secret items** they wanted to keep safe. One, which they wouldn't talk about, was inside the vault. The other, the **missing Enchanted Book,** had been stolen from the massive library.

"Our Enchanted Book is the **only**

one of its kind," Donny said as we arrived at the library, a CLOSED sign hanging from the door. "It's **very, VERY SPECIAL** to the Drowned, and before now, we were the only mob who knew it existed. It's vital that we get it back."

He unlocked the doors and led us in. The library was dark and quiet.

"We've closed the library until our Enchanted Book is recovered," Donny explained. "It contains **powerful knowledge** that cannot fall into the **wrong hands.** No one can know the book is missing—it would

CAUSE CHAOS across the city."

"OOF!" In the darkness, I had accidentally bumped into a small can. It clinked with whatever bits of trash were inside. **"Booby traps."**

"Sorry about that. The cleaners must have left it in the doorway."

Like any good secret agent would, I **sniffed** inside the trash can. I **detected** half a sandwich, a scrunched-up piece of paper, and some broken glass. Maybe someone had dropped a drink bottle or something. Satisfied it was nothing to worry about, I continued following Donny through the library.

"What kind of **knowledge** does the book have that makes it so special?" I asked. "Aren't there Enchanted Books hidden **all over the place?**"

Donny frowned.

"I can't tell you why it's so special," he said. "It's a **DROWNED SECRET.**" He then pointed to a grand **glass case** in the middle of the library, with a label that read

The Enchanted Book of the Drowned. "That's where we keep it."

"In a **GLASS** display case? That doesn't seem very **secure**—wouldn't it be **easy to break?**"

But it *wasn't* broken. There was nothing inside, but the case itself somehow had remained undamaged. All four sides were perfectly intact, as was the top and the bottom. The book had disappeared from inside a sealed glass case—**WITHOUT ANYONE BREAKING THE GLASS.**

A VERY FISHY MYSTERY!

"We Drowned prefer to keep to ourselves, but many **tourists** still visit the Underwater Ruins to see our spectacular library," Donny said. "On the day the book was stolen, a player was here. She came and **examined** this case, and then returned again later. She was here, looking at the empty case, when my security team showed up. So we **arrested her.**"

"How do you think she got the book out of the glass?" I asked.

"Hacking skills?" Brian suggested.

I looked again at the empty case. It didn't look like someone had **hacked** at it with **an ax.** The glass wasn't even cracked . . . yet the book had been extracted somehow.

Donny didn't know how, but he was sure she'd done it.

But something didn't **feel right.** If the player had already stolen the Enchanted Book, why return to the scene of the crime and **WAIT TO GET CAUGHT?** Why would she come back to check out an **empty glass case?**

I inspected the area a little more closely and noticed some **sand** on the floor beside the case. The rest of the library was **spotless.**

"Was this sand here when you

arrested the player?" I asked.

Donny **stared** at me.

"It could have been," he said. "But this is the ocean, Agent Wolf. Sand is kind of **commonplace**."

Fair point, though I couldn't help but **smile**. He'd called me **AGENT WOLF**.

Brian had disappeared at the end of our conversation—**SO RUDE,** just disappearing all the time—but he'd showed up again after a half hour.

"I'm sorry, my mom won't let me play during lunch," he said, shrugging.

"But we didn't have lunch. **And this isn't a game,**" I reminded him sternly. "Donny and his security team have **arrested a player** for this crime."

"It's very mysterious," Brian agreed. "Normally, Enchanted Books are hidden in **Big Ruins Chests** for players to find. I've never heard of one in a glass case that no one can touch."

"This one wasn't supposed to be **found or taken**," Donny said. "It's very special to the Drowned. And we need it **BACK**. Ah, here we are."

Brian stopped in surprise. **"What? JAIL?! But I didn't do anything!"**

"Not for you," I explained while Donny spoke with the security guards. "We're here to interview the **accused player.**"

"**Oh,**" Brian exhaled with relief.

Donny took us to the cell where they were keeping the prisoner.

"These secret agents are here investigating **YOUR CRIME,**" Donny told her through the bars.

"**For the hundredth time, I didn't steal your book!**" she insisted, hands on her hips.

"I was just in the wrong place at the wrong time!"

"It looks like you're *still* in the wrong place," Brian  commented. He shook the bars on the locked door. "Why don't you just **stop playing** so you can get out of here?"

I ROLLED MY EYES. Brian and his games. He didn't seem to understand this was **real life.**

"I can't stop **respawning** in this cell," the prisoner said. "It's like they **corrupted my save.** And they cleared out my inventory, so I need to stay and resolve this."

Brian tapped his chin. "My inventory **glitched** just before we got here. Do you think it was a **global error?**"

"Maybe. These Drowned are a lot more powerful than I'd expected," she said.

"Yes, we are! And we even put **air** in your cell," Donny said with a frown. "You should consider yourself **LUCKY.**"

"What's your name?" Brian asked.

"Quinn," the prisoner said.

"Hi, Quinn. I'm—"

"That's Brian," I interrupted. "And I'm Winston, but you can call me **Agent Wolf.** So, the Drowned security force found you at the scene of the crime?"

"Yes," Quinn said. "I was in the library, and I did see the Enchanted Book, but **I didn't steal it.**"

"Were you there before or after it was stolen?"

"Both. I saw it inside the glass case when I was first exploring the Ruins, and I wondered how I was going to get it out—"

"AHA!" Donny yelled. **"SEE?! GUILTY!"**

"No!" she exclaimed. "It looked impossible to get out without drawing too much attention. Besides, the label said it was a **one-of-a-kind** Enchanted Book that only works when you have its counterpart item."

That caught Brian's interest.

"What item is that?"

We all looked at Donny. He **slapped** a hand over his mouth and shook his head.

He wasn't telling.

"I don't know," Quinn said. "And it's not worth stealing an Enchanted Book if I don't have the item that makes it work."

That made sense.

"Okay, so why **go back** to the library after that?" I asked.

Quinn looked **embarrassed.**

"It's going to sound **CRAZY,** but I was swimming down the hallway after leaving the library when I heard someone say,

'HEY, PLAYER, YOU DROPPED SOMETHING RARE IN THE LIBRARY.'

When I turned around, I couldn't see who'd spoken, but I decided to go back in case I actually had left something behind. That was when I saw the book was missing, and then I got arrested. **I PROMISE,** though, I *didn't* take the book."

It really didn't sound like Quinn had any reason to take the Enchanted Book, but in the short time between her two visits, someone **very quick and crafty** had done it.

"Did you find the rare item you had dropped?" Brian asked.

"No, I checked my inventory afterward. **I *hadn't dropped anything.*"** She shook her head. "I should have checked straightaway."

Hmm, interesting. The real robbers had tricked Quinn into returning to the library. It was a **SETUP!**

"One more question," I said. "Did you notice any **sand** on the ground near the glass case when you visited?"

Quinn thought about it.

"Before the robbery, no," she said. "But after the Enchanted Book was stolen? **YES.**"

We followed Donny out of the jail.

"I don't think Quinn is the thief," Brian announced.

I nodded. MY THOUGHTS EXACTLY!

"I do," Donny said. "**She was at the scene of the crime. TWICE!**"

"But you said that many visitors to the Underwater Ruins come to see your spectacular library," I reminded him. "That means **lots of mobs** were at the scene of the crime. Did anyone **actually see** Quinn break into the case?"

"No . . ." Donny said hesitantly.

"Did anyone see her with the book in her hands?"

"Well, no, but . . . **SHE'S A PLAYER!**"

Brian looked a little **offended,** but I understood what Donny meant.

The wolves were suspicious of players too. And as far as I knew, I was the only one who'd **trusted** a player enough to tame one.

"Just because she's a player doesn't mean she took the Enchanted Book," I countered.

"Players are always **taking things** from around Minecraft," Donny said in annoyance. "They think that if something is lying around, they can **just steal it!** I wonder where she could have hidden it . . ." He kept muttering to himself about dodgy, no-good players.

"I think you're right," I said to Brian. "But because the Drowned have already arrested who they *think* did this, they aren't paying attention to **THE CLUES** that tell us **who the robbers really are.**"

"What clues?"

"The sand, of course! And the empty, sealed glass case, and the mysterious, invisible mob who told Quinn to go back so she would get caught instead of the real thieves."

"If those are clues, what do they all **mean?"** Brian asked.

"How should I know?" I said.

"You're the secret agent!"

"And you're my **junior partner!**
You're supposed to be the one doing
all the hard work collecting clues."

"WHAT?! Why?"

"Because I'm supposed to do all the
cool spy stuff, with my gadgets.
I can't do *everything*."

Just then, a loud alarm **blared**
through the building like a broken
ship's horn. We all blocked our ears.

SCREEECH!
SCREEECH!
SCREEECH!

"WHAT IS THAT?!" I yelled.

"It's the alarm for the **SECRET VAULT!**" Donny shouted, looking shocked. **"Someone is trying to steal our other precious item!"**

We **raced** through the tunnels.
Drowned citizens were hurrying out
of Donny's way, blocking their ears
from the noise. The alarm was **still
blaring** when we reached the vault
door.

"This is the vault!" Donny yelled. We
looked around. The hallway was
empty and the door was **sealed
shut.** "Still locked. Thank the seaweed,

our secret item must be still **SAFE INSIDE!**" He opened a panel beside the door and deactivated the alarm.

"Why did the alarm **go off** if nobody tried to break in?" Brian asked in the silence.

"It must be faulty," Donny said.

Actually, there wasn't *quite* silence. **Tiny bubbles** were streaming from the bottom of the vault wall with faint **popping** sounds.

I leaned in close and saw air escaping through **little holes.**

"I think someone has **DRILLED THROUGH YOUR WALL!**"

"**Nonsense!**" Donny came closer, but soon saw that I was right. The little holes were not coming from any of the other walls, just the vault. "Well, even if someone drilled these holes into our vault, it doesn't matter because they're **too small** for any player to get through. The vault is still sealed."

But I was starting to get **suspicious.** Not every mob is player-sized. Some mobs are huge. And some are **DANGEROUSLY LITTLE** . . .

"What if a **tiny mob** did get in through these holes?" Brian asked. "Could they **sneak** your secret item out the way they got in?"

"Yes, good point, Brian!" I said, looking at Donny to confirm.

"There is only one secret item inside and it is **much too big** to bring through holes this size. You would need to open the door. And since the door has not been opened, the item must be **SAFE AND SOUND**. Anyway, you can't use the item without the Enchanted Book."

Brian and I looked at each other.

"What if the thieves were small enough to get in through these holes *and* had the Enchanted Book?" Brian asked. "Could they use the secret item without taking it out of the vault?"

"Well . . . I mean, I guess so, but they'd also need **metals** for crafting . . ." Donny said.

We looked at the holes again. I could **smell** a lot of different substances coming from the bubbles escaping the vault. Mostly metals.

"Minerals can be **transported** through holes of this size, carried in **small quantities** at a time," I said slowly. "Let's assume that they brought metals with them *and* were small enough to enter through the holes *and* had the Enchanted Book . . . then could the thieves use the secret item without leaving the vault?"

"Um . . . yes. I suppose so."

"**And?**" I encouraged. "That would be . . . **bad?**"

"Yes," Donny agreed. "That would be **QUITE TERRIBLE.**"

"Donny," I said, "what is the secret item inside the vault?"

Donny **sighed.**

I knew he didn't want to tell us anything about the Drowned's big secret, but we had **run out of options**—we had to know!

"You requested help," I reminded him. "That's what I'm here for. Tell me what's so special about the item inside the vault."

"It's the Drowned's **most valuable** secret—our **ENCHANTED ANVIL**," he said. "We use it to craft tridents."

I stared at him. Brian looked confused.

"Wait, **craft tridents?** Tridents aren't craftable in Minecraft."

"Not for players," Donny agreed.

"Why, what do players use anvils for?" I asked.

"We use Enchanted Books and anvils together to **add enchantments** to other items," Brian explained to me. "Like tridents. But I never considered how tridents are **MADE** in the first place."

"That's why it's a secret," Donny said. "The Enchanted Book and Enchanted Anvil are both one of a kind, and we use them to **craft tridents** for Drowned all over Minecraft. If someone else got our precious anvil *and* book, then *any* mob could have our weapons."

"So this is why only Drowned can

spawn with or drop tridents," Brian realized. "Wow. This missing book and anvil are both **GAME CHANGERS!** I wasn't expecting to find such **rare items** on this visit! Do you think I could get a look at the Enchanted Anvil so I can tell my friends?"

"This isn't the time, Brian," I said. "Wait—do you guys **hear** that?"

We all leaned closer to the little bubbling holes.

Chink . . .
Chink . . . chink . . .

We could hear the soft **clanging** of someone working with **metals** inside the vault. Donny looked horrified.

"**Oh no!** The robbers are inside the vault! And they're **USING THE ENCHANTED ANVIL!**"

He **hurried** to the door and tried to open it, but it was still locked. He took keys from his pocket and turned them in the hole, but when he **shook** the door again, it still wouldn't open.

"Why won't it open?" I asked.

Brian and I tried to help pull the door, but it **wouldn't budge!** It was jammed shut!

"I don't know! Maybe I can **override it** . . ." Donny went back to the control panel to check the alarm system while we kept pulling at the door. "There's nothing wrong with the lock mechanism. The robbers must be using something to **bar the door** from the inside."

I got impatient and **banged** on the door with my paw.

"Hey, thieves! **Open this door!**"

"**LET US IN!**" Donny shouted through the little holes. "Let us in so I can **arrest you!**"

"Yeah, *that'll* work," Brian muttered. "Donny, what else is in the vault?"

"Other than the Enchanted Anvil? Nothing."

"And the holes are too small to bring in anything except **very small**

mobs, an Enchanted Book, and some small deposits of metal for crafting, but listen . . ." Brian said.

He tried the door again, and we all listened to the clunking noise it made. When he pulled hard, a **small gap** appeared between the door and the wall.

"I think that they've already started **making tridents,** and they're now USING ONE TO BLOCK THE DOOR FROM THE INSIDE."

Sometimes Brian was pretty smart.

"Okay, then we need to get rid of that trident," I deduced. "What **destroys** tridents?"

Brian and Donny looked at each other.

"Not much," Brian said. "I'm guessing that's why the Drowned use them, because **they're such good weapons.**"

"Yes, that is the reason," Donny agreed. "Also, they **LOOK COOL.**"

He's right. They *do* look cool. And I was starting to think that we were not the only ones who thought so . . .

"**This is a disaster!**" Donny complained. "Our priceless Enchanted Book has been stolen and now it's being used with our special Enchanted Anvil to forge weapons for somebody else. We can't get into the vault to stop them. **And we don't even know who they are!**"

"Actually," I said slowly, "I think I may have **SOLVED THAT MYSTERY . . .**"

"What do you mean, Agent Wolf?" Donny asked.

I grinned. **I'D DONE IT!** I'd solved the case, and I was on my way to **completing my mission.**

"Well," I started, but then—can you believe this?—Brian just ran away. **Swam away.** Whatever. **Right in the middle of my grand reveal!**

I shouted after him, "Can't you wait until **after I've finished talking to disappear? SHEESH!**"

But he didn't come back. I was a little offended, and turned to Donny, my only remaining audience member. At least *he* **looked interested** in hearing how I'd solved the mystery.

"Okay, the first part of the mystery was figuring out how the robbers got the Enchanted Book out of the glass case without breaking it," I said. "But that's just it—**they *did* break it.**"

"No, they didn't. Yes, the book is gone, but the glass case is **still intact,**" Donny said.

"The glass case is indeed still intact with six glass panels . . . but are they all **the original panels? NO!** One of the sides was **broken** so the book could be taken out. We saw the broken glass in the garbage can."

"But how was the glass replaced?" Donny asked. "Nothing is broken now."

"This might be the ocean, but there was sand all around the case and *nowhere else in the library*!" I said.

"The villains broke the glass, stole the book, and **reforged the glass panel** to hide what they'd done."

"I didn't think of that!" Donny gasped. **"THAT SNEAKY PLAYER!"**

"No, Donny, it wasn't a player. Quinn got **tricked** into returning to the library so you would catch the wrong person. Remember she overheard someone telling her she should go back because she dropped something, but when she looked around she couldn't see who had spoken? That's because the speaker was small . . . **AND VERY, VERY CUTE."**

"Huh? Cute?"

"So cute," I explained ominously, "that it **hypnotizes** anyone who sees it."

"The real robbers!" Donny exclaimed, pointing to the tiny holes beside the door. "And now they're in my vault! But I didn't even see them sneak into the city!"

"The hypnosis," I reminded him.

"Your security guys at the front gate probably don't even remember them. They're **crafty** like that."

And once they were inside the city, they could **camp out** for days, or even a few weeks. I thought back to my conversation with old Mrs. Lonewolf. Some mobs carried their homes on their backs. It was like **permanent camping gear—** perfect for a **long-term heist** like this one.

"How many do you think there are?" Donny asked.

"It's impossible to say. While you were busy arresting Quinn and calling for the GUARDs to help over the BARK radar, the thieves had plenty of time to sneak in **reinforcements**. There could be dozens hiding in the vault. Maybe a hundred."

"**A HUNDRED!**" Donny was shocked. "And if every single one of them makes a trident . . ."

"They will have quite the **army** behind this door," I agreed. **IT WAS A WORRYING THOUGHT.**

Donny turned back to the panel on the wall.

"I need to radio for my security team to meet us here," he said. "If you're right, we could be in for **a whole lot of trouble!**" He activated the panel and pressed some buttons. The lights switched off. **"OH NO!** The radio is **broken."**

I came closer to see what was wrong. All the wires for the radio were **chewed through!** Now I definitely knew whom we were up against.

I am a **canine,** after all. I know all about **chewing things I'm not supposed to,** and I would recognize this handiwork anywhere. This chewing was done by **experts.**

"Strong jawline," I noted, examining the bite marks. "No teeth, just a hard, sharp beak for crushing cleanly . . . I'd be impressed if those villains weren't my **SWORN ENEMY.** This heist was carefully planned."

Donny couldn't believe it.

"But what mob could be **small enough** and **evil enough** to hatch such a menacing scheme against the Drowned?"

"Oh," I said darkly. "There is only one mob **SO SMALL AND SO EVIL . . ."**

"BABY TURTLES!"

"Excuse me?"

No one ever took it seriously.

"Baby turtles are the robbers!" I exclaimed. "I know firstpaw just how **villainous** they can be. And they're among the only mobs small enough to squeeze through those holes in the wall to get inside your vault." I hurried to pull at the door again. "We have to **stop them!**"

When Brian and I had fought the baby turtles who'd trapped my wolf friends, they'd all had tridents, and they were very dangerous. But tridents are rare, so the majority of baby turtles wouldn't be armed yet. If every baby turtle all over Minecraft had a trident, that would make it much easier for them to **cause trouble,** and much harder for the wolf GUARDs to stop them.

That is, once the GUARDs actually

started believing me about the baby turtles being the root of all evil in the Overworld. But once we got this door open, I'd have **PROOF!** And my mom and the other GUARDs would know I was right **once and for all!**

"It's still locked!" Donny said. "I don't know how we can **dislodge** the trident they're using to jam the door."

"Why don't we try **heating things up** around here?"

BRIAN WAS BACK! He was

swimming toward us with a heavy-
looking bucket weighing him down.

"Brian! Where have you been? You
missed my **whole reveal!**"

"Let me guess." He landed on the
seafloor beside us. "Baby turtles,
blah blah, bad guys, **blah blah
blah,** Winston figured it out because
he's a genius."

"Actually, that's pretty much it."

"Cool. Or should I say, *hot?* **VERY,
VERY HOT.**" He held up the bucket.
Inside was a glowing, red substance.

Lava! He must have gotten it from the moat around the ruins.

"Let's see if this helps." He went to the vault door and poured the lava through the gap.

HISSSSSSS . . .

On the other side, metal began **dissolving** as the lava oozed all over the trident that was jamming the vault's door shut. Donny and I pulled on the door a few more times, and then **SLAM!** It **burst open.**

The vault was a huge, sealed cavern with a towering ceiling and smooth, stone walls. In the middle of the vault was a platform on which stood a **glittering anvil.** And surrounding that . . .

"**Baby turtles!**" I shouted, leaping over the oozing mess of lava and melted trident. "**NOW YOUR TIME IS UP!**"

A whole squad of baby turtles stood around the anvil, busily crafting small lumps of metal into tridents. Beside them was a **growing pile of weapons**—they must have made close to thirty tridents already! Thankfully, there were fewer turtles than we'd feared. Maybe twelve? Brian, Donny, and I could **take them!**

I activated my Anti-ADORBS collar to prevent hypnosis, and little hearts burst out around me. The first time that had happened I'd been a little embarrassed, but not this time! No, this time **I FELT POWERFUL!**

When they saw me, the baby
turtles stopped what they were
doing and turned to face me.
The leader, who was holding the
Enchanted Book,
pointed to me.

"There he is!"
their leader
squeaked
dangerously.
"The agent wolf
cub I was telling you about. Get him!"

They each picked up a very sharp,
very pointy trident from the pile.
I gulped. I'd forgotten that they

would probably *use* the weapons they'd been working on all day . . .

They began to run toward me.

"Yeah, get him!" Brian yelled. I frowned at him. He was supposed to be on my side! Then he ran up beside me. "And get his friend too. The guy with the **massive bucket of lava!"**

He held up the bucket, and there was still some molten rock glowing ominously inside. It even **sloshed** a little when he shook it, causing a single drop to **spill out.** The turtles stopped suddenly and watched the drop as it fell.

It **MELTED A HOLE** right through the vault floor.

The turtles gulped.

"**NAH, I'M GOOD**," one little turtle squeaked cheerfully. In a blur of bubbles, it **zipped** through the water, swimming directly **over my head** and **out the vault door.**

"**Me too**," said another baby turtle. "**YOU CAN KEEP THE LAVA.**"

One by one, the turtles **chickened out** and swam away, leaving only their leader behind, still holding the Enchanted Book.

"**COWARDS!**" the baby turtle yelled, shaking a **tiny, adorable flipper.** It looked around the vault—at Donny, at Brian's lava bucket, at the big pile of tridents far too heavy for one baby turtle to carry out alone. Then it **glared** at me. "**YOU.**"

"Have we met?" I asked.

Their leader screamed a **terrifyingly cute** battle cry and snatched up the tridents one by one and flung them at me.

Turns out, baby turtles are **very strong** and **very accurate**.

I **dodged** quickly as tridents struck the seafloor all around me.

"ARGH!"

Luckily, Brian was still there.

"**WINSTON, DUCK!**" he shouted.

I quickly did as I was told, falling to the floor and covering my helmet with my paws. Brian **tossed** the bucket of lava over my head and it landed on the pile of tridents. The lava spread quickly, **melting every single one.**

The baby turtle leader had **run out of** weapons.

"You may have thwarted me again, agent wolf cub," it **squealed,** "but next time you won't be **protected** by lava!"

And then it zipped through the water at **impossible speed,** leaving the vault and us behind, the Enchanted Book abandoned on the floor beside the Enchanted Anvil.

There was a very long stretch of silence. Then Donny gasped.

"Seriously?!" he yelled. "BABY TURTLES?!"

"What do you mean, **it wasn't caught on camera?**" I cried in disbelief.

"I mean that nothing was caught on camera." Donny **shrugged**.

"But it's a secure vault! Shouldn't there be **security cameras?!**"

"There *are* security cameras,"

Donny said, "but it seems that the robbers **disabled** those too."

"So you're telling me there is **NO PROOF WHATSOEVER** that the villains who stole the Enchanted Book, framed Quinn, broke into the vault, and used the Enchanted Anvil without permission were **baby turtles?**"

"Uh . . . yeah, pretty much **zero proof,** that's right. But I saw," Donny assured me. "I believe you."

Great. **Just great.** Another mission down, and *still* no evidence to present to my mom and the other GUARDs that our **real enemies** are baby turtles.

"The wolf pack will still think that I'm **CRAZY**," I said in disappointment.

"Look on the bright side, Winston," Brian said, patting my shoulder. "You'll just have to do **another mission** to find your proof!"

I perked up. I hadn't thought of that. Missions are **GOOD FUN**— so this wasn't the worst outcome after all!

"Now that the danger has passed and our precious items have been recovered, I'm going to tell the Drowned about **what you and your player friend did to help us,**" Donny said. "Though, I can't promise that every Drowned will suddenly stop being **suspicious** of players. But the Drowned will be **so offended** by this heist that we will be enemies with the baby turtles **FOR ALL ETERNITY.**"

Two Drowned security came in with Quinn and **unlocked** the handcuffs on her wrists.

"I'm sorry we kept you **locked up** before we knew for sure who the robbers were," Donny said to Quinn. "Your **inventory** has been released and should be restored. You can **respawn** wherever you like now."

"Thank you," she said. Then she turned to us. "Thank you, Agent Wolf. Who knows how long I might have been **stuck in that cell** if you hadn't **solved** the mystery."

"Hopefully, it'll **never happen again**," Brian agreed. "Donny, will you be **improving security** around the vault and the library to prevent further robberies?"

"**DEFINITELY**," he said. "We were inspired by your **use of lava** to scare off the baby turtles. I guess no one likes the threat of being **melted.** We just need to think about how to build the lava into the vault's protections."

"I'm actually something of a **builder** myself," Brian said. "I could help you with **planning out** the new security design, if you like?"

"Me too," Quinn said. "I'm a pro! Once I spent **a whole month** building myself **an island."** Just like Brian earlier, Quinn suddenly grabbed a door out from **NOWHERE** and stuck it in the sand so she could take a few breaths.

"Wow, really?" Brian said. "Building is one of my **favorite parts** of playing Minecraft."

I rolled my eyes. Again with the *playing.* One day Brian was going to have to grow up and realize **LIFE IS NOT A GAME!**

But I supposed it was okay to let him have fun every once in a while. I'm a good **pet owner** like that. I smiled patiently while Brian and Quinn **excitedly** discussed the merits of different designs and different building materials. Then Donny offered to show them the best places to find the materials they would need.

"Give me a moment before we go," Brian said to Donny and Quinn. He turned to me. "What are you going to do now, Winston?"

"The case is **solved** and the mission is **completed,** so this secret agent is heading back to the Den."

I was quite **PROUD OF MYSELF.** Even though there was still no evidence that baby turtles were the source of all evildoing in Minecraft, at least I had **helped the Drowned,** made new friends, and completed my mission.

Well, **almost.**

"We'd better **return this,"** I said,

holding up the Enchanted Book. I'd picked it up off the vault floor after the baby turtle's leader had dropped it. "Would you like it back in the library, Donny?"

"Yes, please," he said. "One of the librarians will **take care of it** and make sure it gets back inside its glass case. Maybe Brian and Quinn can come up with **ideas** of where to put security as protection in there too."

Brian's trick had made Donny very **keen on lava!**

"Good idea," I said. "But I'll also talk

to my mom—ah, High Commander Wolf—about sending out a team of GUARDs to help as well. They're very **experienced** at this kind of thing."

And maybe the GUARDs could **learn a thing or two** about baby turtles from listening to what Donny had to say.

"It was fun **adventuring** with you again, Winston," Brian said as we swam back to the library. "Although maybe next time we can take a mission **above sea level?**"

"I'm afraid the secret agent life

takes me to **ALL KINDS OF PLACES,** Brian," I said.

At the library, we found a librarian and she put back the Enchanted Book in its glass case.

"The Drowned are very grateful for everything you've done," she told us. "In fact, we even have a **small gift** for you." She offered me a little present.

"That's **too kind,**" I said, shaking my head. "But a secret agent **DOES NOT ACCEPT PRESENTS.** I'm a professional."

"To be honest, I'm not sure *whom* it came from," she said, "but it has your name on it. **To: Agent wolf cub.**"

I frowned and had a look. Nobody ever called me that, *except . . .*

To: Agent wolf cub
From: Your nemesis

SEE YOU SOON . . .

I gasped. The leader of the baby turtles was **TAUNTING ME!**

"What's inside?" Brian grabbed the present and unwrapped it.

"**Be careful!** It could be **DANGEROUS!**"

But inside was a glinting, blue–and–yellow crystal. It looked like **a star.**

"**A NETHER STAR!**" Brian exclaimed. "But what do you think it means?"

"It means," I said thoughtfully, starting to feel **excited** again, "our next mission is calling us, and it's **definitely above sea level.**

What do you know about
THE NETHER, Brian?"